Zephyr TAKES Flight

STEVE LIGHT

CANDLEWICK PRESS

Zephyr loved airplanes.

She drew pictures of them,

made them out of paper,

and built them out of junk.

Mostly, she played with them.

One day, she hoped to fly one of her own.

"Grandma! Look at my plane!" Zephyr shouted.

But Grandma was reading the paper.

"Daddy, play airplane with me!"
said Zephyr.
"Not now," said Daddy.
"I'm busy."

Zephyr went to find Mom, but she was busy, too.

So Zephyr tried her **triple loop-de-loop spectacular**

off the couch.

CRASH!

Zephyr was in trouble.

In her room, she folded a paper airplane and sent it zipping
through the air. It landed behind the dresser.

There was something
back there!

It was a door. . . .

This was surely the most wondrous place Zephyr had ever seen.

It was filled with papers and pens, drawings and maps,
books about how to fly and where to go.

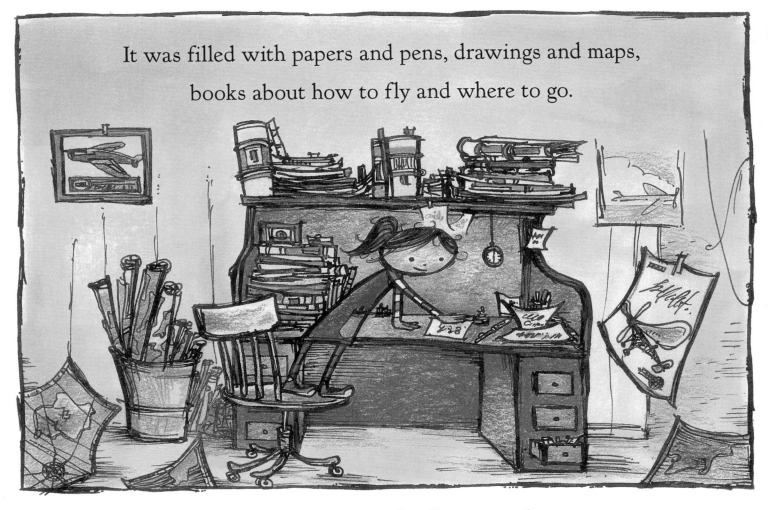

And then there were the flying machines.
There were big ones and small ones, some with propellers and some
with rudders and very strange things. And all of them were real.

 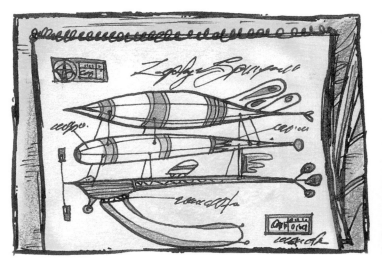

Zephyr had an idea. . . .

She climbed aboard the FS *Bessie*. She flipped the switches.

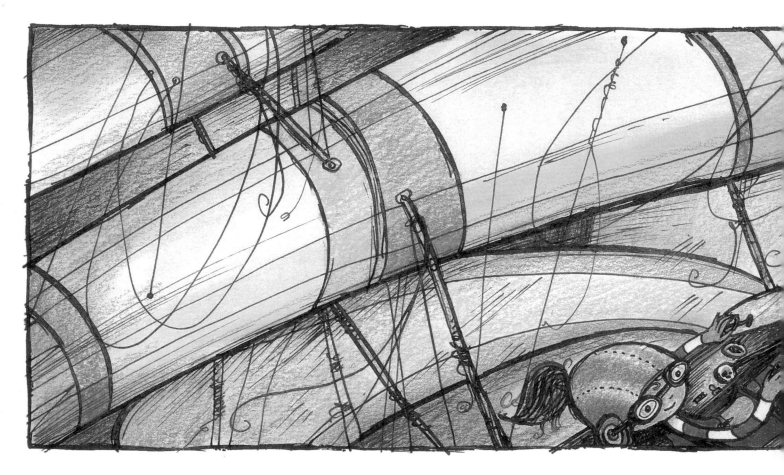

The engine creaked and cranked and finally started up.

Her **triple loop-de-loop spectacular** was much more

fun in the sky!

Putt-putt, sputter-sputter.

Oh, no!

The engine coughed and went quiet.

The FS *Bessie* drifted lower and lower.

Zephyr held on tight.

BUMP!

The plane landed. *What is this place?* thought Zephyr.
She had never seen mountains so high, skies so blue, trees so lush.

And in the distance . . .

flying pigs!

As Zephyr hurried toward the village,
one small pig ran along beside her.

The little pig said his name was Rumbus.

He could not fly.

Zephyr felt sad for the little pig.

Flying was a wonderful thing!

Then she had an idea. . . .

Zephyr measured
and folded.

Zephyr drew
and cut.

Then Rumbus
took a running start . . .

and he flew!

"Do a
**triple loop-de-loop
spectacular!**"
called Zephyr.

Zephyr was happy to see Rumbus fly with his family
for the first time.

Zephyr thought of her own family.

It was time to go home.

She'd need help from her new friend.

Rumbus had an idea.

Zephyr ran to breakfast and had a . . .

triple-hug, triple-pancake spectacular!

To Mia and Emily — my inspirations for Zephyr

First edition 2012

Library of Congress Cataloging-in-Publication Data is available.

Library of Congress Catalog Card Number pending

ISBN 978-0-7636-5695-9

12 13 14 15 16 17 SCP 10 9 8 7 6 5 4 3 2 1

Printed in Humen, Dongguan, China

This book was typeset in Kennerly.
The illustrations were done in pen and ink using a Pelikan M1000 fountain pen with added ink flow by Richard Binder
and a Mont Blanc 149 fountain pen. They were then colored using PanPastels and Prismacolor colored pencils.

Candlewick Press
99 Dover Street
Somerville, Massachusetts 02144

visit us at www.candlewick.com